Every X Has It's Y

Once 'X' s'l was someone

21^2X, And when I finally met you

Published By

Every X has it's Y

Edited by Rashmika

ISBN (Paperback) - 9788194928829

First Edition : 2021

Book Design by POETRY WORLD

Every X Has It's Y

Once 'X' s'l was someone

$2l^2X$. And when I finally met you

Compiler & Editor

Rashmika Aitha

Rashmika Aitha

Rashmika is a voracious consumer of the written word, who always has a book(or a Kindle, keeping with times) by her side that she devours. She is a student aiming to reach the peak and have a glimpse once. Rashmika moonlights as a here her nostalgic side seeps through her blogger w words. She is inclined towards micro tales and poems but secretly harbors a dream of writing a novel.

Instagram: - @RASHMIXX06, @rashmikaialfazz

Gmail: - rashmikamss7@gmail.com

INDEX

Aditi Khera

MY EQUATION WITH MATH

Maths was numbers all I knew

But they added alphabets too

Even then, I was fine

Y's (whys) were o and A's (grades) were nine.

They told to prove triangles' congruency,

Wished to scream "why prove, can't you see"?

But was blessed with teachers good

And I learned how it should.

Sin, cot, cosec, woke me from the dream,

So math's isn't that easy, as it seems!

Integration and limitations were mom's fear,

Scared too, I chose to leave the subject there.

Give me 4-3 digit calculations, I was quick and good

But with CA, There it stood.

What I boasted, gives me a laugh

With calculators I do, double and half!

Neither Shakuntala Devi nor Aryabhatta,

I ever wished to be.

But I often regret and miss,

My equation with Math was happy!

Akshat Gupta

MOVE IN MATHS

Aao tumhe pyaar ka Ganit (Maths) sikhate hai,

Aao tumko ye batate hai 1 =1+1 kyu ho jate hai ,

Are byahi toh saccha pyaar hai,

Jo do jism aur ek jaan khalate hai

Aur tabhi i sb X = Y kehlate hai …

Ananya Malhotra

MATHS, O MATHS!

In addition, subtraction was fine

Good to go into the head of mine

Multiplication and division came next

And I titled math's as the Best

Growing up, I came to realize

That math's was necessary to become wise

Equations and formulas were a must

To quench the petty examiner's thirst

And so I tried and tried and tried

And in this process, my brain indeed got fried

I dived deep into the ocean of numbers and digits

And started understanding math's in bits and bits

Soon it became my favorite subject

And getting full marks, I didn't become deject

But now, as I am in grade eleven

I spend on it, hours seven

Still, I get confused a bit

Regarding how the solution, I should knit

Now it has become the ardent archetype of study

So, I request you to practice it, my buddy

Because math's is a very vital part of our life

As it teaches us to practice, to win strife

Math's! I adore you for you are unique

And I pray that your respect doesn't become bleak!

Anchal Singh

MATHEMATICS: A PURE MAGIC!

Do you know why I love mathematics?

Because math is pure magic.

I know it never tells us to add or multiply happiness and double our joy nor it tells us how to subtract sadness and bad memories from our life.

But it tells us something, and that is every problem,

every tough question has a solution.

Those mistakes can happen and they can

also be corrected.

In real life, we get simple problems

but make it complex.

And we all have seen it in our lives, that calculations and equations whether it's about people or things in life are more difficult than the problems

of mathematics.

Mathematics tells us that even if we get into trouble, we can fix it. We just have to start it again; we have to try and try to find its solution with a different method.

And that's why I love it.

Ankita dwivedi

MATH

Math's or hm...

Ji math's ek aise balaa hai ji ke aag me hmne 10 saal
jala hai.....

Math's or hmari banti nhi.

Kyu ki meri or iski baat jamti nhi...

Ye x or y me lga rehta hai..

Or hmara Dimag 11-2-9 ho jata hai...

Jaha start hui iski Π waha mujhe nind aayi...

Ek baat hme aaj tk samjh naa aayi is matha ko kisi ne
ban kyu nhi lgayi...

Math's ek aise balaa hai ji ke aag me hmne

10 sal jala hai..

Arpita Khare

LANGUAGE OF MATHS

Strictly speaking, a language is a verbalized means of communication, enabling the speaker to convey thought to another person. However, the more complex the thoughts or ideas, the harder or more cumbersome language becomes. To explain verbally why 'the square on the hypotenuse of a right-angled triangle equals the sum of the squares on the other two sides' would require a long and tedious paragraph or great math tutors. So in this way, mathematical symbols which nowadays are universally accepted, compress information in a way that no ether 'language' possibly could, and this fact supports the topic statements.

However, this 'language' is only available to most people in its simplest forms, i.e. arithmetic, algebra, and geometry, and these are taught in schools because they have everyday usage. In this sense, of course, mathematics is a minority language, a language intelligible only to the specialists of all nations.

Mathematics has been described as 'the spearhead of natural philosophy', and this was certainly true up to about 1800. The subject grew up independently in China, India, the Arab world, and Europe. For example, many of the Alexandrian and Greek schools of geometricians, represented by Thales of Miletus, Pythagoras, Euclid, Archimedes, etc advanced propositions which were already Pythagoras, Euclid, Archimedes, etc advanced propositions which were already known elsewhere.

Descartes revived algebraic geometry, Napier invented logarithms, Newton and Leibnitz the calculus. Lobachevski developed non-Euclidian geometry and was followed by Einstein, though the latter was more of a physicist than a mathematician. From Newton onwards, mechanics and astronomy began to use advanced mathematics, and later on, physics came in for the same treatment.

So mathematics has become a 'beautiful language' in several senses. Firstly, in its ability to compress ideas, just as a great poet achieves desired effects by the great verbal economy. Second, because it's tools, the symbols, are internationally accepted. Third, because it is entirely objective, and completely exact, allowing no room for prejudice or human emotion. Fourth, because it constantly provides the ground for new hypotheses.

Mathematics means 'facts', verified by experiment, and these facts are true within the four dimensions in which the human mind can operate. The other dimensions, perhaps six according to Stephan Hawking, must be compressed into infinitesimal space, so are likely to remain the prerogative of the Creator!

Ayushi Tiwari

SQUARE OF X

Square of X is expanded when

Or squeezed having an error

Always unseen to the naked eyes

Vibration continues in the earth

X is X, error too little one

X square adjustable everywhere

The matter of oiliness' a matter

Of change, loneliness the feelings

Found with a big group even in scatter.

X, not now X in this Universal sphere

X square adjustable with the squeezed

Or expanded up to the reach where

Feelings of X, the realization of X differ

Only to assume the access of miracle

So-called MAYA, the expansion itself

The shade of a body in presence of light

Otherwise X square stands like a limit

The universe, thoughts of a mind state

X square, the square of X anywhere

Stays with the error inside the mindset

Beyond or within the sphere of our thoughts.

Baisakhi Das

MATH IS A GAME

Math is a game

Full of fame

Around the world, it is played

Where problems are to be solved

Even English alphabets are involved

Where some problems are easy to solve

While other difficult ones revolve around our head, giving

stress wanting to take rest

In this game, everyone is forced to play

Some sit at bay

Not willing to attend the play.

Bansari Parikh

OPEN LETTER TO MATHS

Dear Not So Good, But Scoring Subject,

Yes, I am talking about you only, Math's. How shall I start with?

Let me start with your variations. Sometimes you just give us myths in form of AXIOMS and sometimes, sometimes you just give us a headache by finding your X. Like what can a person like me do? Algebra, Circle, Geometry, Ratios...ah! My life ratios have been unstable since forever with you. You tell us to find you're X with respect to your Y and we get our answers in Z. How ironic right? And yes, those rounder's and compass box filled with scales, and what not just were so trendy back then. We used to have them with us always, no not because we loved geometry, but because we loved playing with those things.

How have you been lately? Are there more students like me who hate you but sometimes love you too? I have been away from you for like ₄ years now and trust me whenever I see you now, I feel so easy to solve you and your problems. Maybe because of time or maybe because of our long journey.

Dear math's,

I miss you, I miss to have those "mam can I solve this question on board?" times. You were the only one who never told me to mug up things. And you were the one who taught me the practicality of life. Thank you, I know you are shocked to see that your hater writes an open letter to you, but just those few time things when hate isn't hated anymore.

See you on some other beautiful side, yet again keeping rounder on middle and drawing shapes and finding answers with Pythagoras theorems.

Till then see you!

Keep students stress free, please.

Chahat Kanchan

RELATION OF X - Y

Everyone has the incomplete equation X

And before writing the equation next

The addition of love

The elimination of hate

In the hope, they come back

We always wait

The multiplication of explanation

You give it to them

They divide the care

They go somewhere

You do not know where and when

The Y is another level

Depict in equations

X+Y = 0 is

The general explanation

So all vanish away

When they ADD together

They still stay Far away if

We square them whether

The linear line graph

How much you want the high

You never ask why

Still, Every X has in this equation only "Y".

Chakshu pahuja

MATHELOPHOBIC

Sin by Cos is equal to tan,

Whatever it is math's is my phobia man,

Algebraic equations are easy to solve,

But when I look at them my heart and brain revolve,

Teachers said, follow the rule BODMAS always,

Who would tell her I won't even get an answer following

the rule that ways,

To avoid math's I took medical happily,

But there say physics - M friends with math's majorly,

Every x has a y, and the known axis is x y and z

Probability was easy but maths said m not that probable

to buzz,

People solving an equation and saying it was easy,

My heart throbbing faster when am not able to solve but
wondering to keep myself busy,

*Books seemed a headache and always a fear of failing
in math's exam,*

The fear was too severe just after gym you get the
muscle cramp,

*After 10th I thought I was relieved but differentiation
integration still didn't give me peace,*

Now I realize how long I try to run from it, but basic
maths of gains and losses should not be ceased.

Whatever happens, my phobia is goanna remain,

For plus-minus, I need a calculator except

for my brain.

Chinsha Bhatia

I FELL FOR NUMBERS

I fell for numbers,

When I got a hundred in class first

I fell for numbers,

When we sang tables together

With a crowd of teachers

And students around

I fell for numbers,

When I feel fine

When we studied theorems

From RD Sharma in class nine

I fell for numbers,

When choosing math's with commerce

To do the actuary course

Sound so rare

I fell for numbers,

When I practice a lot

And find it so much interesting to float!!!

Christy Gnana Deepa.J

EVERY BEGINNING HAS AN END

Mathematics, my favorite subject,

And occasionally it's hectic

Paramour of formulas,

Hidden formulas within lovers.

Every beginning has an end,

Every X has its Y.

Each formula has a special significance,

And it has a perfect coincidence.

Taste the formulas of Math's,

With your lovely path.

Deepanshi Khatri

FEAR OF MATHS

For whom doing math's can be fun,

It's only practice and nothing to learn.

Who can love math's as a subject,

I'm candid so I confess.

Getting passing marks in this subject

was my only goal,

And to fulfill these flying chits

played a significant role.

I tried to get passing marks to my level best,

But unfortunately, in the exam, I ended

up making a mess.

My fate never cooperated with my endeavor,

And my marks were never in my favor.

Then, at last, I ended up quitting maths,

Then, at least I ended up quitting maths.

Dharshinipriya.R

DEAR MATHS

From day one we met,

I have a crush on you,

I don't know when it changed as love, and now you

became a core of my life...

Dikshita parashar

KALEDIDOSCOPIC LOVE

Hugged by fire, betrayed by rain..she was in such a kaleidoscopic love that it washed her away. Nothing remained, except her ashes..but if you take your eyes off it, she'll make you soaked in the summer rage of revenge that runs through her burned veins. One of the biggest mistakes was mixing those ashes with the pen's blood //the ink// that painted her as living poetry in between dead pages so quickly. Whenever you read poetry, remember it's a deed's portrait that remains as a curse between those pages.

Dishaben Patel

THE NUMBERS

Once Upon a time, there was a number

Pure and round as the sun

But alone too alone

He began to reckon with himself.

He divided and multiplied himself.

He was removing himself.

And he was always alone.

He ceased to reckon with himself.

And closed in the round

Soar's purity

The fire was left outside

Traces of his accounts

They started chasing each other in the dark.

To divide when they had to multiply

To be removed when they needed to be added

These things happen in the dark

And no one could be found to tell him.

Stop the traces

And erase them...

Dr. Chittepu Nithisha

A LETTER TO MATHS

Oh, my dear mathematics...

I know u since I was born

From remembering the day of my birthday

For these many years, I have been living on this earth till

today.

Be it in remembering dates of events...

Or in the expenditure of life.

U was there with me.

Right from scoring marks in individual subjects to get a

decent total...

To eliminating the calculated risks of life...

U was there.

Some took u as a career and some made u a part and
parcel of their life.

Though I couldn't travel all along with u...

I had never left u alone...

I was never scared of u...

In fact, u never made to do so...

U was there even in the worst times...

When I wasn't prepared at all...

U took me close to u

And made me perform well.

I knew theorems better

That was from how I learned theories of life.

I was always proud that I knew u better

Then a science student

May be less than an engineering student.

But on a scale of human being, I know u

Pretty well.

I know if u are my X...

I will be your Y...

So that combination equals Z.

Even when divided by someone...

The change is none.

- From a friend of math's.

Geethika Reddy

MATHS CLASS

My one and the only hateful subject is Math's,

I usually plan to escape out of this class,

I feel so boring and scratch my head,

Those 3d shapes will see my face and laugh

at my death,

Multiplication will be adding more numbers,

I usually feel Math's is the world's biggest trumpery,

By using geometrical instruments I will be

putting rangoli,

I feel that wontedly this idiotic time is walking slowly,

Those sums lie on the page in order,

For me, Math's phobia is a great disorder,

When my Math's sir call me by my name to do a problem
on board,

*I feel so awkward and struggle a lot to win this battle with
a sword,*

Those percentages and fractions,

Always make me fight with those interactions,

Even now I hate Math's and Math's class,

Solving those equations made me wear eyeglass,

I do get the first class in each and every subject,

*But I don't know why I always get second class and it
always deflects me.*

But moreover, the thing which we hate,

Is the only one which we love the most?

Gurleen Kaur

ANSWER IS NEVER FOUND

I played with every digit,

Becoming a friend with formulas,

Finding the areas.

Loving the shapes,

Triangles, squares, rectangles

Even the circle which is round,

But the answer is never found.

I don't know Y (Why),

Maybe it's my X (Ex),

That's why it's hiding from me.

Studying Algebra for hours,

Needs a lot of power.

Its equations became my most favorite,

I got confused with my math's relationship,

Whether it's of love and hate.

Plus, Minus, Divide, and Multiplying,

All feel like they are flying.

Again and again,

Turning everything around,

But the answer is never found.

Hema Kirthiga J

THE KILLER SUBJECT

Why the algebra?

To kill me!

Why the fraction!

To burn me alive!

Why the integral?

To slap my face!

Why the coding?

To make me insane!

Why the Venn diagram?

To help me pass!

Why the age problem?

To bury me!

Why math?

To kill me.

Ilaiya Kanmani R

MATHOPHILIA MIND

The World is cool with numbers!

Here the life revolves around,

The Four major operations.

We add people of our interest,

With multiple desires.....and

Subtract them when we lose the heat!

Divided among ourselves.....

Yet probabilities are way more with positivity,

Uniting people and set off their functions.

Shapes and lines are life curves,

Teaching ups and downs.

Every shape has its measure!

The World seems attractive and energetic,

When visions are practical,

About the life calculations!

Until we choose to solve this inevitable necessity,

It appears a problem to ye all!

#eye of a math admirer.

Ipsita Panigrahi

THE LOVE OF MY HEART...!!!

Mathematics is not just a subject.

It's a thing that makes me reflect.

It's the love of my heart and more than emotion to me.

It enlightens my darkened paths and

Help me to shine and glee.

It's a text of facts and proofs.

It completes the home of science without roofs.

It's a game of certainty.

But you know ...the exception is probability!

It's a family of relations and sets.

Where trigonometry and geometry brawl for bets.

Algebra and arithmetic were most loved

in this mÉnage.

Derivation and integration have disliked the

hell as garbage,

Because dealing with these things need

a lot of courage.

Integers are the naughtiest one.

Who is always in the mood of doing fun?

Sometimes it goes with positive, sometimes

it goes negative.

Though it's a family member it acts as a

distant relative.

Each and every member of this family makes me happy
from the inside.

No matter how much I feel low.

It never leaves my side.

53

Mathematics is the king of all.

It's the point guard in the game of basketball.

Without this everything on this earth will cease.

They help to unbolt the lock of every field,

As they are the most desired keys.

Jayashree Sahoo

LOVE FOR YOU IN MATH

When you enter my life suddenly,

All problems of my life solved equally,

When your cares and jokes added to my life by plus,

Then my woes with tension distracted

my life by minus,

When you love me too deeply from your inner heart,

I just divide your love in a fraction for loving

you more bit,

Always I want to love you more than me,

But you always be first and love more,

Than me,

When you hold my hand smoothly,

My feelings attract toward you equally,

Multiplying your more love, I find a solution,

That our love always pure and full of dedication.

Jyothsna Sontyana

BE MY 'X'

Will you be the x to this y?

Help me to find myself by substituting

You and lemma equal it to "Love" to

Make a beautiful equation "US".

Jyoti Singh

LET IT BE 'X', IRONICAL MATHS

The confusion was always on peek,

Math's since school has increased my heartbeats,

I used to scratch my minds to find the answers in the chaos of problems of Math's,

Let it be 'x' was one of the most annoying of all packs.

Ironical Math's

I stayed away as knew the subject was not my play,

Ironical Math's however found the precious bond,

My best friend had the for the tray in Math's,

Though I stayed away from the Subject but got stuck my heart with her.

Kajal Mittal

MATHEMATICS : A SWEET

NIGHTMARE !

Dear Math's,

Are you aware of the fact?

Your existence makes me regret,

For having you as a compulsory subject,

People say you're logical,

Then why you seem to be so illogical?

To my life, thank you for adding so much stress,

That I forget how I would subtract all this mess,

You've doubled the time for me to practice my test,

I wish if I could divide it well & manage the rest.

O my loving math's,

It's been so complicated with you always,

For now, I've started having a phobia & want to break up

your legs!

O my loving math's,

My heart manifests,

Please leave me alone,

For both of us that would be the Best!

Krishna Motwani

MATHS IS LOVE

Math's is what I love,

What I feel,

What I think,

What I do with happiness and concentration.

Some of the students think that Math's is boring, I don't

love Math's, I can't do it, I can't solve that sum and many

more expressions come on their face when they solve

any of the sums.

But Math's is not that hard,

We just have to concentrate while doing it.

We should take interest in that,

We should think that how this/that sum you

can solve easily.

The main reason behind that why I love math's is...

Because it gives me peace,

Because I solve patiently,

Because I feel something unique,

That's why I use to show more interest to know more
about each and every topic in math's.

When I do addition,

I feel like I am adding more happiness to my life.

When I do subtraction,

I feel like I am subtracting some sadness from my life.

When I do any of the sums,

It just gives me happiness,

It just gives me some special feel.

　　　　　　　　　　　　　

Math's is X and I am his Y.

I love Math's much more than any of

the other subjects!

I love Math's much more than any of

Kritika Sharma

DILEMMA

Yesterday my cousin asked a question about

mathematics,

I felt horrible just like a lunatic,

I asked my brother to solve the equation,

Just like a pro, he solved it in a single operation,

I wonder how a single subject can have

so many variations,

One loves that thing and other

experiences palpitations,

Everyone is afraid of something,

I have a fear of this mathematics string,

Whenever I see an expression I feel very shy,

I always imagine why every X has its Y,

People who love this subject are really lucky,

I want to learn it but I have a fear of this...

Lavisha Vinayak

MATHS

Something like this is a song of remembrance

As much as I like you, I miss you,

Equally, I get careless about myself,

My memory of math's is enough now,

When I subtract myself from you,

I'm left with zero.

Mausam Agrawal

MATHS IS LIKE A COIN

Like a coin has two sides

The same is maths in real life

For someone, it is 100 on 100 deals

For someone even passing is a dream

Some attend the classes

To impress their upcoming X

And for some, the teacher is the first love whom they

need to impress

Messages are passed by saving in the calculator

And some feel the passing is a burden.

Math's is a subject

Which scares and helps

You can be friends

And it will never leave your hand

It can be an enemy too

Which destroys all the equations?

Of your life.

It can solve your problems and can always be

at your side

Megha Maheshwari

ME AND MATH...

As the bell rang my heart broke into pieces this horror is of math's or maybe of my math's teacher this is still a dilemma for my little brain for which math is like a horror movie or a pain which can't be expressed in words...

This story is about my 10th class...

When I scored good Mark's more than my expectations or even my teacher's expectation. I gave a Hope to my teacher to score better Mark's in my half-yearly and what happened was unexpected!! You all will not believe, My confidence has ruined everything. Maths had —always been my enemy and YES, this time too...You may call it's a phobia for me

"Math's Phobia"...

I have never scored well in math but as far as I remember I did once...and scoring well in math was like achieving something bigger...

The story of math and I will never end!!

Though I am not a writer, still I tried to explain my relationship with math...

Nesba Sahir

X AND Y IN MATHS

Without X, the Real part of the graph will show

syntax error.

Without Y, the Imaginary part of the graph will show

syntax error.

Without X, the Quadratic equation will show

syntax error.

Without Y, the Circle equation will show syntax error.

Without X, Sin x Cos x will show syntax error.

Without Y, Tan y cot y will show syntax error.

Without X, the Congruence property will show

syntax error.

Without Y, the Set function will show a syntax error.

Without X, Constant will show syntax error.

Without Y, the Subset will show syntax error.

Without X, We can't solve anything.

Without Y, We can't get any answer.

Without math's,

Life is like a

X and Y.

Nobil Initha J

I MET MR. X AND MR. Y IN MY LIFE

I met Mr. X as a solution

I met Mr. Y as a converter

They danced in my answer sheets

The illusion of mathematics captured me

My fingers start to count out

To place Mr. X as a solution

And he invites digits of numbers as guests

To justify him as a solution

My calculator blabber with answers

Of different digits to place Mr. Y

To justify him as a converter

In life conversion and solution

Is the practice in one life?

To add you're subtract of failure

As a division of lessons

To multiply success!

Prachi Gupta

MATHEMATICS

I solve questions,

I solve arithmetic's

It's hard to crackle algebra

But it's easy to find it's X.

I take my pen and start

Proving the riddle

I solve a problem in an hour or a day.

It's not hard to solve geometry

But it's not so easy

To find the answer to every query.

I just like to tackle obstacles

That's why I love mathematics!!!

Pragya Verma

NO TO MATHS

Mathematics, the name is itself dangerous,

Its x and y's are fully disastrous.

In childhood, I love to do maths every time,

Addition and subtraction were joyful as rhymes.

Trigonometry, differentiation, and integration,

Made my life as hectic as the situation of this nation.

NCERT questions were not solvable,

My fear of maths was unstoppable.

In childhood, we used to shout ,1,2,3,4

But now, I don't want to see them anymore.

This phobia is untreatable,

As for me, math's is unsolvable.

I used to love it, when I get to solve one question,

But after that, every question gives me tension.

I said no to math's because I had no solution.

Pragyan Panda

SOLUTION TO EQUATION

Life's full of calculations;

We ought to find our solutions!!

*Maybe a straight line_*

Or in an elliptical revolving Earth;

Maybe a repeating circle;

In a confusing parabolic path.

Irrespective of positive;

And negative slopes:

We need to move with our vibes;

And happy hopes.

Often curved and clumsy with real;

Also confused and mislead by imaginary,

We are supposed to distinguish artificially

And get off from every misery.

Pratham Mittal

MATHS FEAR

Numbers, numbers, everywhere

Some consider them as a boon,

Some exerting to overcome them

Others just don't care.

Math's fear they assert

And are content, but Hey!

Don't they know that it's cowardice?

To be lazy and tell lies?

Nothing is too difficult to overcome,

Nothing too wild to tame,

Everything needs hard work

And nobody else should be blamed.

So the next time you're haunted,

And by just a few numbers taunted,

Just shrug and smile,

And reply in a cool style.

I'll never be afraid,

I am here to remain.

To conquer these numbers,

yes, I'll give my best till I'm grayed.

I would never hand over,

Won't ever leave,

Till numbers are conquered and beneath my feet.

Priyanka K Goswami

MATHS PHOBIC

To prove is another hilarious session,

Differentiation and integration are their compassion...

You may decide with logarithm's fate,

Drawing figures in geometry is like their true

soul mate...

Being Tan Cos and Sin is real fun than algebraic,

So trigonometry is love for all math's phobic...

Go with confusing arithmetic or jump into

a deep matrix...

Go solving equalize polynomial or fly high in

graphic statistics...

Being a mathematician is great fun to fly high,

As every X has its Y...

Rohit Gupta

YOU AND ME

If I'm your Trigonometry, You are my Geometry Dear

If you are like Circle, I'm the Centre here

If you are like Coordinate Plane, I'm your Axis there

In the Math's of our love life, we are like Algebraic

stars near.

Roshini Aitha

CHANGE IN MATHEMATICS

Dear maths,

Stop giving us stress,

We are fed up with your ex(X)

Now, we are happy to please you just move to the next.

Your ex(X) has given us a lot of pain but doing all this

there is no gain in our vein.

Dear math's a small request to you,

I am very sick finding your ex(X) just accept the fact, that

she has gone, and you just move on to dude.

Sahaj Sabharwal

STAY COOL (POETIC RAP)

Stay cool,

Don't be a fool,

Just like a mule,

Are you a dull stool?

Never be in terror loon,

Or you will see an error soon.

Do something new,

Which is done by a few?

Always be in the mood,

Your attitude should never be rude,

As for advice by Sahaj, my dude.

Make your own rules,

Use them as necessary tools,

And consider your opposes as big fools,

Take proper rest till your mind cools.

Sakshi Jain

MATHS – A PHOBIA

Try, try and try,

The more I try,

The more I cry.

I practice math's with my heart and soul,

Yet I am not able to achieve my goal.

I never get marks in math's,

Despite my great endeavors

Fate is never in my favor.

I want to improve my math's, because I love the subject,

and for this, I am trying my level best.

I am candid so I confess,

in mathematics examination

I always create a mess.

All the answers I guess

and ultimately the marks I get are quite less,

I believe that if I do ample practice

I'll one day probable achieve my goal and

I seriously have to improve, because in our lives math's

has a very significant role.

Sakshi Saxena

X HAS ITS Y

*The view of the playground with children playing from
dusk to dawn*

I feel like making it a memory full of joy- filled

with crayons

Suddenly the sheets flow and ink dropping mimicking the
chaos in me

*And the problems pile up in front on the board and
numbers were the only thing I could see*

Every step was a challenge with infinite efforts required
to reach the top

Once done with it, I felt like I should never stop

These lessons were the stairs of my life on which I
dream of walking as step by step learning to strive

I remember how I used to cry for this twisted yet

interesting thing, till I understood that every

X has its Y.

Shalini Kevat "Shehzadi"

HENCE PROVED

Be the one you are,

Let me suppose you "x";

I promise you to be your

"Y" in all your dark and light phases.

I will complement you being with you all my life,

We will prove "x=y";

I think it's "Hence Proved" that you are going

to be mine.

Sherya

GEOMETRY

I think that I shall never see...

A book as lovely as geometry.

A book between her covers preset

Assumptions, theorems, and the rest.

A book that in her binding holds

A nest of old papers between her folds.

Upon whose pages pens have written

Whose back binding a dog has bitten.

A book that into my locker goes.

Who intimately lives with my gym clothes

Poems are made by fools like me,

But Euclid made geometry.

Simar Dhiman

THE LIMIT DOES NOT EXIST

Math's is defined as a preposterous, horrible, frustrating, disgusting, and boring subject where anything can happen at any anytime without even a single logic. Attending a math class is like watching a Chinese movie without subtitles. No matter how much you practice you will always get a boiled egg on your test. It is just like a drama queen who is full of Solution fewer problems. The biggest contributors to this pointless subject are the lost case Mr. X (who due to some mental disorder) always forgets its value, the high profile criminal Mr. Sin (belonging to the murderous trigonometry planet), numbers which appear as dancing spiders, the compass hurting as a stabbing knife, the positive and negative sign (who have the supernatural powers to disappear), long filthy calculations, the never-ending list of stupid theorems, rot learning of formulas, irrelevant Corollaries, the endless Mr. Pi, the snake of math's Mr. Integration and the biggest depression for all the students that is the angle of depression. There is no limit to this mental torture. Three ways to solve a math's problem are:
1) *Write down the question*

2) Stare at it continuously

3) Start crying

Oh god, save our future generations from these deadly curses!!

Suhita S

94

SMARTEST !

World's only smartest person who tackles

the problems

By his methods and disciplines

Moreover with his delighters

Making all others follow him eventually!

Swapna S. Tripathy

MATHS – LOVE & SCAR TOO...

"Mathematics is the science that deals with the logic of shape, quantity and arrangement. Math is all around us, in everything we do. It is the building block for everything in our daily lives, including mobile devices, architecture (ancient and modern), art, money, engineering, and even sports". It is the definition whom we are using since the birth of maths. Use to formulate new conjectures; they resolve the truth or falsity of such by mathematical proof. When mathematical structures are good models of real phenomena, mathematical reasoning can be used to provide insight or predictions about nature. Through the use of abstraction and logic, mathematics developed from counting, calculation, measurement, and the systematic study of the shapes and motions of physical objects. Practical mathematics has been a human activity from as far back as written records exists. The research required to solve mathematical problems can take years or even centuries of sustained inquiry. Mathematics developed at a relatively slow pace until the Renaissance when mathematical innovations interacting with new scientific discoveries led to a rapid increase in the rate of mathematical discovery that has continued to the present day. It has a natural number, fraction, polynomial, algebra, Euclid geometry, Trigonometry, construction, etc. Math has its value in life. Every x has y as a solution, but if you don't know the solution that how to get the answer of y, then it's a scar. Math has its importance and uses in day to day life. There's the value of square, cube, Π ,$\sqrt{\ }$ etc. It has addition, subtraction, multiplication, division to simplify the question. BODMAS rule is very useful. It has value in Physics too.

Swayamdeepta Das

MY FIRST LOVE-MATHS

Math's phobia-a very familiar problem

encountered by students

Quite fortunately, I haven't faced it and all the credit

goes to my mother

From the very beginning of schooling,

She tried to teach me in such a manner

That I fall in love with the subject

Students begin fearing a subject when

They fail to understand the basics

This ultimately weakens their foundation

Mother always tried to make difficult

concepts easier for me

Math's needs regular practice so she

Ensured that I never procrastinated

She helped me discover the utility of the subject in
day-to-day life

This enhanced my interest in it.

I could sit with the math's book for hours together

Without getting bored, strange? No.

If you practice math's only to score marks

You may find it tough, but if you practice

For discovering the beauty of the subject

It will develop into your favorite, trust me.

Vedika Agrawal

MATHS – SOMETIMES LOVE REST PHOBIA

Math's the one which comes to the brain but never into
the heart,

The one which is never permanent,

Never stable and secure for its existence in mind,

*But when practiced and understandable nothing is
divine.*

Aarti gupta

गणित का डर

दिलचस्प थी वो गणित कीं किताबें ,

मेरी बचपन की जुड़ी हैं उससे काफ़ी यादें।

सबसे पहले हमें सिखाया गया था जोड़,

जिससे दूर भागने के लिए हम जाते थे दोड।

फिर अध्यापिका बोली इन अंकों का कीजिए घटाव ,

हम भी बहोत बेशर्मी से बोले ,

आप ऐसे फ़िज़ूल कामों का दुनिया से ही कर दीजिए
मिटाव।

फिर वो बोलीं दो गुणा दो कितना ,

हमने कहा ,आप लोग हमसे ये चीज़ें करवाकर हमें

तनाव में क्यूँ डालते हैं इतना।

फिर विभाग का भी सवाल आया ,

तब दिल बेचारा बोलने को मजबूर ही हो गया ,

ये गणित किसने बनाया।

ये तो ख़ैर बचपन की बात थी ,

जब ऐसे फ़ालतू विषय से हमारी पहली मुलाक़ात थी।

आगे आगे बढ़े तो ट्रिगनामट्री आया ,

उसका ज़िन्दगी में क्या लाभ है ,अल्लाह

क़सम आज तक समझ नहीं आया।

नींद की गोली की ज़रूरत नहीं थी हमें ,

केवल गणित की किताब खोल लेना ही नींद

लाने के लिए काफ़ी लगता था...

और अगर एक भी सवाल सुलझा लेते थे हम,

तो हर बच्चा अपने आपको पूरी

कक्षा का ज्ञानी समझने लगता था।

बस कुछ ऐसी ही थी कहानी हमारी ,

ये गणित जैसे फ़ालतू विषय में घसीटटे-घसीटटे निकल

गयी स्कूल की आधी जवानी हमारी।

Ashima Jain

कौन सी संख्या है सबसे महान

होड़ मची संख्याओं के बिच ,है कौन सबसे महान

किसकी पूजा हो पहले ,किसकी हो पहले पहचान

सब अपनी करते थे बड़ाई ,फिर उनमें हो गई लड़ाई

किसी की बुद्धि काम न आई ,फिर सबने मिलकर सभा बुलाई

जज बने युनिवर्सल दादा ,इम्पटी ,सिंगल्टन ,पेपर ,सबसेट

सब थे मध्य मौजूद ,अकड दिखाकर जीरों बोला

अपनी वकील हूँ मैं खुद

संख्याओं ने तब कहा विनय से-

हे युनिवर्सल दादा ! जरा करें हग सबकी पहचान

जीरों अकड रहा है कब से ,दिखा रहा है जूठी शान

मुच्छ पर अपनी ताव देकर अकड़कर फिर जीरों बोला -हाँ हाँ हाँ

जिस पर मेरी नजर बढ़े ,हो जाए वो मालामाल

जिस पे मेरी नजर चढ़े ,पल में कर दूँ उसकों कंगाल

आगे किसी के जब लग जाऊं ,एक को मैं दस बनाऊ

अगर पीछे कभी ना आऊ ,फिर मैं उनका भाव घटाऊ

भाग लगे जब किसी को मुझसे ,खजाना हो उसका अनन्त

गुणा करो जब किसी किसी को मुझसे ,कर देता उसका अंत

जन्म हुआ भारत में मेरा ,पूरे विश्व ने अपनाया

Banna govardhan raj purohit

एक्स कहु या वाय!.....

चलो उसके ख़्वाबों में ले चलुँ

कुछ अपनी कुछ उसकी

आज में सरे आम दासतां कहुँ

कुछ अनोखीं...

कुछ प्यारी है...

दिखने वो सबसे न्यारी है

हाँ करू तारीफ़ किसी दूसरे की

"तो बेवफ़ा मुझे कहती है"

हाँ ! वो कुछ इस-तरह है ,

जो खोई-खोई सी रहती है

सांवली सी है पर प्यारी है

थोड़ी ही सही पर सबसे न्यारी है

थोड़ी ही देर में वो सबसे घुल जाती है

इस बेगानें जहाँ में उसकी यही बात तो निराली है

बस उसको देखकर मेरी आँखें खुलती है

उसके मिलने पर ही मेरी

"बस शाम औऱ सुबह होती है"

एक" चाय "ही तो है जो मेरी रग-रग से

घुल मिलकर अपने होने का एहसास दिलाती है!...

ये प्रेम नहीं तो क्या है जो मुझे उसका अपना बनाती है!...

Chahat Bajaj

MATH ATTACK

प्लस माइन्स के फनडे हर मंडे

याद दिलाते मम्मी के डंडे

गणित का विषय क्यो है इतना जरूरी

ये है एक बड़ी भारी मजबूरी

पास हो जाओ इस बार

हाथ जोड़े है कितनी बार

किताब से निकलते $\cos\theta$ के वार

करते मेरे होंसले को तार तार

कब होगा ये सम सोलव

कर लिए जी तोड़ प्रयत्न

बारह साल तक झेला है

ये कभी ना खतम होने वाला समुद्र मंथन

Deepti Rana

एक्स(X) की वाई(Y)

आज हम बात करते ह एक लड़की की कहानी की ,जो गणित से दोस्ती करते करते दुश्मनी कर बैठी थी। ये कहानी है उस लड़की अंजानी की मैथ्स ,बहुत कम लोगों का पसंदीदा विषय होता है ,और वो उन कुछ लोगों में से तो बिलकुल नहीं थी। वो क्या है न मैथ्स में वो शुरू से ही बस ठीक-ठाक थी।   दसवीं बोर्ड की परीक्षा में उसने ९० प्रति शत के साथ नॉन-मेडिकल लिया,अब जैसाकि आप सब लोग जानते ही हैं की नॉन-मेडिकल में मैथ्स मुख्य विषय होता है तो ये उसके लिए एक चुनौती साबित होने वाली थी उसे ये तो पता था ,मगर कितनी बड़ी इसका किसी को कोई अंदाज़ा नहीं था। अपना पसंदीदा विषय लेने के लिए उसने स्कूल बदला था। ग्यारहवीं कक्षा में शुरू-शुरू में उसमें बहुत उत्साह था पर जब उसकी पहली इकाई की परीक्षा हुई और उसके अंक कम आये तो उसने और मेहनत करने की ठानी किन्तु फिर भी लगातार उसके कम अंक के कारण उसे ऐसा

लग रहा था मानो वो जैसे खुद को हारते हुए देख रही हो। इन सब के चलते उसका अंतर्मुखी होना उसके लिए एक बहुत बड़ी समस्या बन चूका था क्योंकि उसके अंतर्मुखी व्यवहार के चलते उसे किसी से मदद लेने में भी बहुत संकोच हो रहा था और ये उसे और मुश्किलों में डाल रहा था। उसने किसी तरह ग्यारहवीं की परीक्षाएं तो पार करली थी मगर असली चुनौती तो अब थी। उसकी ये दुविधा उसके घरवालों से भी छिपी नहीं थी और इसके समाधान के लिए उन्होंने उसके लिए अच्छे से अच्छे अध्यापन की सुविधा मोहिया करवाई किन्तु इससे भी उसकी ये मुश्किल हल नहीं हो रही थी। वो इस बात से बिलकुल अनजान थी की ये सब देख रही थी उसकी मैथ्स की अध्यापिका श्रीमती पूनम। अधियपिका पहले तो चुप रही और इंतज़ार करती रही की कब वो उनके पास अपनी समस्या ले कर आए परन्तु उसके ऐसा न करने पर अधियपिका खुद उसके पास आयी और उसे पढ़ना शुरू किया। जहाँ एक तरफ बच्चे मैथ्स के आसान पाठ पर ध्यान दे रहे थे अधियपिका ने तब उसे उसकी कमियां और ताकत बताते हुए वो पाठ करवाए जो उसकी ताकत बन सकते थे। जहाँ कभी वो मैथ्स इसलिए नहीं

पढ़ती थी क्योंकि उसे लगता था की मैथ्स उसे आता ही नहीं है आज वो मैथ्स दिल लगा कर पढ़ रही थी सिर्फ उसकी अध्यापिका की वजह से। अधियपिका हर बार उसे बोलती "बेटा तुम्हें सब आता है ,बस खुद पर विश्वास रखो " अधियपिका के उस विश्वास ने उसे जिंदगी की सबसे बड़ी चुनौती का सामना करने की हिम्मत दी। अगर मैथ्स की भाषा में बोले तो लड़की एक्स(X) थी जिसकी वैल्यू सिर्फ वाई(Y) मतलब मेउसकी अध्यापिका की वजह से मिली। वो इस एक्स (X) की वाई (Y) बन कर आयी और सब ईकुअशन हल हो गयी। अनजानी

Dil ki feeling 143

IT'S A SCARY TALE

नन्ही-सी उम्र में

ना जाने कितने खौफ बनते हैं

भूत प्रेतों का खौफ

तो कहीं इन से

भी खतरनाक खौफ

अंको का खौफ

गणित का खौफ,,।

खौफ तो खौफ

जिस दिन गणित की परीक्षा होती थी

उस दिन तो मानो

डर से हाथ पैर सुन हो जाते थे

और मन तो रब से खुदा से

एक ही दुआएं करता था

या तो यह परीक्षा गायब कर दो

या गणित को ही गायब कर दो स्कूल से

ना यह गणित रहेगा

ना गणित की परीक्षाएं हुआ करेंगे,,,।

बचपन का वह कोमल सा मन और उस पर यह खतरनाक

गणित का खौफ है,,,

वह जिंदगी...।

Mohd Sahil

MATHS PHOBIA

मैथ्स का डर रेहता है सब में

कोई दिखाता है तो कोई छुपाता है सबसे

ये मैथ्स का बनाते है खौफ

जैसे ये मैथ्स नहीं ,है कोई डॉन

जब मैथ्स का पीरियड आता तो बढ़ जाती धड़कने

किसी के पेट में दर्द तो किसी के सिर में दर्द

मन में रेहता था कि टीचर होजाए बीमार ,

बेमतलब जब घंटी बजती तो पता चला अजादी का मतलब।

साइन कॉस टैन सेक ना आए कभी काम

ना जाने इन्हे पढ़ के हमें मिला क्या इनाम?

पीटने के डर से

रट के जाते थे सारे फॉर्मूले

रट के सुनाते थे और फिर भूल जाते थे यही फॉर्मूले।

एरिया ऑफ ट्रायंगल ,पेरेमीटर ऑफ सर्कल

ये सब नहीं बना पाए अच्छे दोस्तों का सर्कल।

ये बोलते थे ,ज़िन्दगी में मैथ्स आएगी काम

पर अभी भी है उस वक़्त का इंतजार

ज़िन्दगी में मैथ्स बस इतना है कि-:

ज्ञान को गुना) × (करो

गमो को भाग (-) करो

खुशियों को जोड़ा (+) करो

और खाने को बाटा) ÷ (करो।

Nisha Sharma

गणित ना समझ आई मुझको

गणित समझ ना आई मुझको,

गणित समझ ना आई मुझको,

हर सवाल में रुलाई मुझको,

गणित समझ ना आई मुझको,

X की संख्या,

Y का बेर,

Sin की दही,

Cos की खेर,

गणित बुलाई मुझको,

हर हाल में हल कर मुझे!

कहकर डांट लगाई मुझको,

गणित समझ ना आई मुझको,

भौतिक विज्ञान रानी इसकी,

राजा बन फिर चिडाई मुझको,

गणित समझ ना आई मुझको,

सभी विषय अध्यापिका समझाई मुझको,

मगर गणित तब भी समझ ना आई मुझको।

Ruma Begam

Y=m*x+c

जो कभी मेरी लाइफ की y=mx+c हुआ करती थी ,

अब वो मेरी2 x/2 हैं।

2018की एस.आर.के दिमाग वाली सुनले तू वी ,

अब मेरे पास12 x/2x पैक्स हैं।

ग्राफ पेपर जैसी इउनिट में डिवाइड कर गई थी मेरी दिल को।

शुक्रिया तूझे वी ,कुच नहीं तो ∞

जैसी बढ़ा गई मेरी सेर्बि बिल को।

तेरी झूठा y=1/x, x^2+y^2=9, y=|-2x|

और x=-3|siny| की चक्कर में जान गंवाने बेटी थी।

तेरी सेपरेशन की ग़म में ,बिना मौत के कब्र किनारे लेटी थी।

ओबटिउस एंगल जैसा ,राइट ना होने पर में वी डिप्रेस्ड था।

शायद मुजेसे तेरी प्रबाबिलिटी ऑफ सेटिशफिकसन जिरू

था।

तेरी पेयर का किताब ,

मैथ्स की किताब जैसा हि प्रॉब्लम ही प्रॉब्लम था।

पर सारी प्रॉब्लम की इकूएसान को में ने वी दोनों तरफ

जिरू से मल्टीप्लाई कर दिया था।

कहानी पूरी कार्लो में ने ,जो तू अधूरी छोरके गई थी।

अब मात लौट ना हमदर्द बनके ,

क्यूंकि में ने वी मैथ्स में पीएचडी कर रखी थी।

Sarabjot Purba

गणित की शिक्षा

पढ़ने को मन करता है ,

गणित की शिक्षा होती प्यारी।

समझदार बनाता सबको ,

बढ़ाऐ दिमाग की शक्ति हमारी।

जब सवाल हल करते है ,

दूनिया भूल जाती सारी।

गणित तो पढ़ना आसान भी नहीं ,

होती है एक जिम्मेदारी।

किसी को अच्छा लगता ये ,

किसी पर हो जाता भारी।

कुछ ने पढ़ना छोड़ दिया,

किसी का गणित आज भी जारी।

गणित का कहना है हम सबको ,

जिन्दगी बना सकता हूँ तुम्हारी।

गणित भी उनके पास ना जाता ,

जिस किसी ने लात है मारी।

जिन्दगी में सबके काम है आता ,

वो हो अमीर या हो भिखारी।

गणित की शिक्षा मिलनी चाहिए ,

इसने ही सबकी जिंदगी सुधारी।

Shivani Yadav

गणित का खौफ

मुझे ज़िंदगी का वो पल आज भी याद है,

मुझे गणित का वो खौफ आज भी याद है,

कैसे गणित के सवाल मुझे डराते थे,

कैसे आज टेस्ट ना हो उसकी दुआए हम मांगते थे,

गणित के टेस्ट में अंडे भी मिलते थे,

ओर हाथों पर डंडे भी पड़ते थे,

अरे बस 10 वी तक तो झेलनी थी,

बस दिल में यही एक तस्सली थीं,

जैसे तैसे वो वक्त तो गुज़र गया,

लेकिन अपने साथ एक सीखने का जूनून ले गया,

काश इतना डरना नहीं चाहिए था,

थोड़ा डर से लड़ना चाहिए था,

लेकिन असली गणित तो ज़िंदगी खुद हैं

जहां सकारात्मक विचारो को जोड़ना है,

और नकारात्मक विचारो को घटाना हैं,

ओर खुशियों का गुणा कर ज़िंदगी की गणित को सरल
करना हैं।।

Shivika Sharma

गणित के किस्से

जब हम छोटे थे,

तो गणित के नाम से रोते थे।

और जब हम बड़े हुए,

तो और भी ज़्यादा रोने लगे।।

बहुत लोग डरते है,

गणित के विषय से।

बहुत लोग पीछा भी छुड्डाना चाहते हैं,

गणित के विषय से।।

लेकिन बचपन से ही मुझे,

ये विषय बहुत ही पसंद था।

मुझे गणित को बनाने में,

बड़ा ही मज़ा आता था।।

लेकिन जब गई मैं ग्यारहवीं में,

कुछ लोगों के कहने से मैं इसे नहीं ली।

मेरा अंक हमेशा से ही,

गणित में अच्छा रहता था।।

आज भी पछतावा होता है,

कि मैंने गणित को क्यों छोड़ दिया।

इसलिए विनती है सबसे कि अपने जीवन का फैसला,

केवल खुद से लेना ,दूसरों के द्वारा नहीं।।

Siya Ray

125

तुम्हारा मुझे यु छोड़ जाना लाजमी था कयोंकि जनाब हम math student है 'x' तो हमारे किस्मत मै लिखा होता है।

तेरे साथ है मेरा इश्क कुछ गणित सा,

थोडा उलझा हुआ थोडा मुश्किल सा।

Vaishali Soni

में त्रिभुज का कोई सवाल सा ,

वो पाइथागोरस प्रमेय मेरी,

में नील बट्टे सन्नाटा,

वो क्लास की टॉपर मेरी!

Mathematics is not always about solving
problems.

Sometimes we have to assume wrong things
as right and prove that our assumption is
wrong.

129

Every X has its Y　Poetry World Org.

130